D1741089

THE CURLY-HAIRED
HEN

CONTENTS

CHAPTER I

MOTHER ETIENNE'S FARM

"Oh Grandfather, tell us a story, do. You know, the one you began the other evening about Mother Etienne's big farm. You remember. The weather is so bad and we can't go out. Go on, Grandfather, please."

Coaxingly the three children clung round their grandfather, looking at him beseechingly. He adoring the children as he did, loved to hear them plead.

At last he began:

Since you have been very good, and you want it so much, I will tell you the wonderful story of Mother Etienne's farm and the still more wonderful story of what happened to one of its occupants.

Love animals, my children, be kind to them, care for them, and you will surely have your reward.

Mother Etienne was a good stout woman with a very kind heart. While still young she was so unfortunate as to lose her husband and her son of whom she was very fond. This made her, as you can imagine, very, very sad. She wouldn't listen to any new offers of marriage though she had plenty of them. Instead, she devoted her life, her whole existence, to the attentive, nay I ought to say, the maternal care, of the animals on her farm, making them as comfortable as could be.

She had, as I said before, a most excellent heart, the good Mother Etienne. You shall see that presently.

This good woman then lived on her big farm, very spacious and admirably situated. A slate roof covered the large house; the granaries, stables and outhouses were sheltered by old thatching upon which grew moss and lichen.

Let me tell you now, dear children, who were the chief occupants of the farm. First there was big "Coco"—a fine Normandy horse—bay-coloured and very fat, whose silky coat had a purple sheen; he had a star on his forehead and a pink mark between his eyes. He was very gentle and answered to the voice of his mistress. If Mother Etienne passed by his stable he never failed to scent her and whinnied at once. That was his way of showing his friendliness and saying,

"Good morning."

His good mistress spoiled him with all sorts of dainties. Sometimes a crust of bread, sometimes a handful of carrots, but what he loved best of all was sugar. If you had given him a whole loaf he would soon have eaten it up.

Coco had for stable companions three fine Swiss cows. Their names were La Blonde, Blanchotte, and Nera. You know what the colours were for the names, don't you?

Petit-Jacques, the stable boy, took care of them. On fine days he led them to pasture into a bog paddock near the farm up against a pretty wood of silver beeches. A large pond of clear water covered one corner of the meadow and lost itself in the reeds and iris. There the fine big cows went to quench their thirst; quantities of frogs went there, too, to play leap-frog. It was a veritable earthly Paradise.

From the farm Mother Etienne caught the sound of the large bronze bells each with its different low note, which hung round the necks of the cows; thus she could superintend their comings and goings without interrupting her various occupations. For the farm was very big, as I told you, and had many animals on it.

After the stables and coachhouses came the piggery, the rabbit hutches, and finally an immense poultry-yard divided into a thousand compartments, and sheltering a whole horde of poultry of all sorts; fowls of all kinds and of all breeds, geese, guineafowl, pigeons, ducks, and what all besides. What wasn't there in that prodigious poultry-yard?

Mother Etienne spent most of her time there, for the smaller and more delicate the creatures the more interest and care she gave them.

"The weak need so much protection," this excellent woman would say, and she was right.

So for the baby ducks her tenderness was limitless. What dangers had to be avoided to raise successfully all these tiny folks!

Did a pig escape? Immediately danger threatened the poultry-yard. For a pig has terrible teeth and he doesn't care what he eats—he would as soon crunch a little duckling as a carrot. So she had to watch every minute, every second even. For besides, in spite of the vigilance of "Labrie," the faithful watchdog, sometimes rats would suck the blood of the young pigeons. Once even a whole litter of rabbits was destroyed that way.

To dispose of the products of her farm, Mother Etienne drove twice a week to market in her market-cart drawn by Coco.

She was famed for the best vegetables, the purest and creamiest milk; in short, the eggs she sold were the freshest, the poultry and rabbits the tenderest and most juicy to be had. As soon as she and Coco came trotting into the market there was a rush to get to her first.

There, as everywhere, everyone loved Mother Etienne.

CHAPTER II

A MOTHER'S DEVOTION

Thus time passed peacefully at the big farm.

One day, however, the quiet was disturbed by a little drama which convulsed the calm but busy spot.

Mother Etienne had given to a Cochin-China hen, which she had christened Yollande, some white duck's eggs to sit on. The batch of fifteen eggs had all come out. It was really wonderful to see these fifteen baby ducks, yellow as canaries, beaks and webbed feet pink, swarming around the big patient sitting mother, ducking under her wings, to come out presently and clamber helter-skelter onto her broad back. As often happens with nurses, Yollande loved the ducklings as her own children, and without worrying about their shape or plumage, so different from her own, she showered upon them proofs of the tenderest affection. Did a fly pass within their reach, all these little ones jumped at it—tumbling in their efforts to catch it. The little yellow balls with their wide-awake air never took a second's rest.

Well cared for and well fed, they grew so rapidly that soon they had to have more space. Mother Etienne housed them then on the edge of the pond in a latticed coop opening onto a sloping board which led down to the water. It was, as it were, a big swimming bath, which grew gradually deeper and deeper. The ducks and geese loved to plunge in and hardly left the water except to take their meals.

Yollande felt very out of place in this new dwelling. The ducklings on the contrary, urged on by their instinct, madly enjoyed it and rushed pell-mell into the water.

This inexplicable impulse terrified their mama. She was, in fact, "as mad as a wet hen."

She ran up and down, her feathers on end, her face swollen, her crest red, clucking away, trying to persuade her babies not to venture into the water. For hens, like cats, hate the water. It was unspeakable torture to her. The children would not listen; deaf to her prayers, her cries, these rascally babies ventured farther and farther out. They were at last and for the first time in their favourite element, lighter than little corks, they floated, dived, plunged, raced, fought, playing all sorts of tricks.

Meanwhile, Yollande was eating her heart out. She rushed to and fro, keeping her eyes glued on the disobedient ones. Suddenly she saw a mother-duck chasing her darlings. This was more than she could bear,—driven by her maternal instinct she leapt like a fury to the aid of her family.

A flap or two of her wings and she was above the water into which she fell at the deepest part.

Splashing,—struggling madly in the midst of her frightened brood,—she was soon exhausted and succumbing to syncope, she sank to the bottom.

The surface of the water closed above her. The little ones did not realize what had happened—very quickly recovering from their momentary fright, they went on with their games—splashing the water with their beaks and amusing themselves as though nothing were the matter.

Mother Etienne, busy giving green apples to the pigs, bran to the rabbits, and corn to the pigeons, came back presently, and could not see the big Yollande beside the pond, only her children floating far, far away on the water. Surprised she drew nearer, called, but in vain. The mother-hen had disappeared. Then only did she understand the tragedy that had occurred. She called for help. Petit-Jacques immediately opened the big sluice and the water ran out, but much too slowly for their impatience. At last they began to see the bottom, and soon the body of poor Yollande was discovered stiff and motionless.

There was general consternation at the farm. Petit-Jacques, by means of a long pole, seized her and drew her to land at Mother Etienne's feet. Labrie came up and sniffed sadly at the body of the unhappy hen. In vain they dried her and rubbed her,—nothing did any good.

"She's quite dead, alas," said Mother Etienne with tears in her eyes, "but it was my own fault. I ought to have closed down the lattice and this misfortune would not have happened. It really is a great pity—such a fine hen. She weighs at least eight pounds. There, Germaine, take her and weigh her."

Germaine was the maid and also the cousin of Petit-Jacques—of whom she was very fond. She was a fine buxom girl of eighteen, strong and well-grown. She loved animals, too, but her feeling for them could not be compared to Mother Etienne's.

"Germaine, take away poor Yollande, I am quite upset by this trouble. You will bury her this evening, in a corner of the kitchen-garden—deep enough to prevent any animal digging her up. I leave it to you—do it carefully."

The girl bore away the fine hen in her apron. "How heavy she is—it is a shame," and blowing apart the feathers, she saw the skin underneath as yellow and plump as you could wish. Mechanically she plucked a few feathers.

"After all," she said, "it isn't as though she had died—she was drowned, quite a clean death; she's firm and healthy, only an hour ago she was as strong and well as could be. Why shouldn't we eat her?—We'll stew her because, though she is not old, she is not exactly in her first youth—but there's a lot on her—with a dressing of carrots and nutmeg, a bunch of herbs and a tomato, with a calf's foot to make a good jelly, I believe she'd make a lovely dinner."

Saying this she went on plucking Yollande. All the feathers, large and small, gone, a little down was left, so to get rid of this she lit an old newspaper and held her over it.

"Madame won't know anything and will enjoy her as much as we shall. There's enough on her for two good meals."

Quite decided, instead of burying her, she wrapped the future stew carefully in a perfectly clean cloth and put it on a shelf in the kitchen out of the way of flies or accident.

During this time Mother Etienne was busy making as warm a home as she could for the fifteen little orphans. Poor darlings. In a wicker-basket she covered a layer of straw with another of wadding and fine down. Upon this she put the ducklings one by one, and covered the whole with feathers; then closing the lid, she carried the basket to the stable where the air was always nice and warm. All this took time; it was about six o'clock in the evening, the sun was going down, throwing a last oblique smile into the kitchen, gleaming here and there on the shining copper which hung on the walls.

CHAPTER III

YOLLANDE'S TROUSSEAU

As for Germaine, she, with Petit-Jacques to help her, had gone to milk the cows. Mother Etienne soon joined them, and the two women came back to the house together.

Horror of horrors! What a terrible sight. Pale with fear they stood on the threshold of the kitchen not daring to move—to enter. Their hearts were in their mouths. A ghost stood there in front of them—Yollande—and Germaine fell at Mother Etienne's feet in utter consternation. Yollande? Yes, Yollande, but what a Yollande! Heavens! Yollande plucked, literally plucked! Yollande emerging from her shroud like Lazarus from his tomb! Yollande risen from the dead! A cry of anguish burst from the heart of kind Mother Etienne.

"Yollande, oh, Yollande!"

The Cochin-China replied by a long shudder.

This is what had happened.

On falling into the water, Yollande after struggling fiercely succumbed to syncope, and her lungs ceasing to act she had ceased to breathe, so the water had not entered her lungs. That is why she was not drowned. Life was, so to speak, suspended. The syncope lasted some time. The considerable heat to which she was subjected when Germaine held her above the flaming newspaper had brought about a healthy reaction and in the solitude of the kitchen she had recovered consciousness.

After the first moment of terror was over, Germaine confessed her plan to Mother Etienne, who, glad to find Yollande still alive, forgave Germaine the disobedience which had saved her.

But the hen was still shivering, shaking in every limb, her skin all goose-flesh. Dragging after her her travesty of a tail, she jumped onto the kitchen-table which she shook with her shivering.

"We can't leave her like that any longer," said Mother Etienne, "we must cover her up somehow," and straightway she wrapped her up in all the cloths she could lay her hands on. Germaine prepared some hot wine with sugar in it, and the two women fed her with it in spoonfuls,—then they took a good drink of it themselves. All three at once felt the better for it. Yollande spent the night in these hastily-made swaddling clothes between two foot-warmers which threw out a gentle and continuous heat and kept away the catarrh with which the poor Cochin-China was threatened. The great question which arose now was how they were to protect her from the cold in future. Both of them cogitated over it.

Several times during the night, Mother Etienne and the maid came to look at the hen, who, worn out by such a long day of fatigue and suffering, at last closed her eyes, relaxed, and slept till morning.

Nevertheless she was the first in the house to wake up, and at dawn began to cackle vigorously. Germaine hastened to her, bringing a quantity of corn which the hen, doubtless owing to her fast of the day before, ate greedily.

Now the important thing was to find her a practical costume. The weather was mild but there was great danger in allowing her to wander about in a garb as light as it was primitive. The mornings and evenings were cool and might bring on a cold, inflammation or congestion of the lungs, rheumatism, or what not.

At all costs a new misfortune must be avoided. At last they dressed her in silk cunningly fashioned and lined with wadding. Thus garbed her entry into the poultry-yard was a subject of astonishment to some, fear to others, and excitement to most of the birds she met on her way.

In vain Mother Etienne strove to tone down the colours of the stuffs, to modify the cut of the garments, but Yollande long remained an object of surprise and antipathy to the majority of the poultry.

The scandal soon reached its climax.

"That hen must be mad," said an old duck to his wife.

"Just imagine dressing up like that; she'll come along one of these days in a bathing suit," cried a young rooster who prided himself on his wit.

A young turkey tugged at her clothes, trying to pull them off, and all the others looked on laughing and hurling insults . . . They vied with one another in sarcastic speeches. At last, after a time, as the saying goes, "Familiarity bred contempt." The fear which her companions had felt at first soon changed into a familiarity often too great for the unhappy Cochin-China. They tried to see who could play her the shabbiest trick. Hens are often as cruel as men, which is saying a great deal.

Poor Yollande, in spite of her size, her solidity, and strength, nearly always emerged half-dressed. Her companions could not stand her dressed like that, the sight of her irritated them. Not content with tearing her clothes they often pecked at the poor creature as well.

Mother Etienne did her best to improve these costumes in every way—but it was as impossible to find perfection as the philosopher's stone.

They hoped at the farm that in time the feathers would grow again. Meanwhile it was hard on the hen.

Nothing of the sort happened; one, two, three months passed and not the least vestige of down appeared on the hen, who had to be protected like a human being from the changes of climate and so forth. Like a well-to-do farmer's wife Yollande had her linen-chest and a complete outfit.

It was, I assure you, my dear children, kept up most carefully. There was always a button to sew on, a buttonhole to remake, or a tear to be mended. Thus constantly in touch with the household Madame Hen soon thought she belonged to it. Indeed, worn out by the teasing of her companions, by the constant arguments she had with them, and touched on the other hand by the affectionate care of her mistresses, Yollande stayed more and more in the house. Coddled and swathed in her fantastic costumes, she sat in the chimney corner like a little Cinderella changed into a hen; from this corner she quietly watched; nothing escaped her notice.

Meanwhile her reputation had grown, not only amongst her comrades, but amongst all the animals of the neighbourhood, who, hearing her discussed, were anxious to see her.

Woe to the cat or dog who dared venture too far into the room! Very annoyed at this impertinent curiosity, she would leap upon the importunate stranger and punish him terribly with her sharp beak. Of course he would run off howling and frightened to death. It was very funny to watch.

Mother Etienne and Germaine were much amused at these little comedies, and whenever visitors came to the farm they would try to provoke one. Everyone enjoyed them hugely.

Germaine treated Yollande like a doll. She made her all sorts of fashionable clothes. The Cochin-China would be dressed sometimes like a man, sometimes like a woman. She had made her quite a collection of little trousers and vests, which had style, I can tell you. She had copied, too, from a circus she had seen, an English clown's costume which was most becoming. Nothing could be funnier than to watch this tiny dwarf, to see her strut, jump, dance, coming and going, skipping around suddenly,—one moment skittish, the next very important.

Petit-Jacques loved to tease her, but not roughly; he would push her with his foot, and make her jump at him impatiently, looking perfectly ridiculous in her quaint dress. You could have sworn she was a miniature clown. Add to all this, the queer inarticulate sounds she made when she was angry, and even then you can have no idea how very amusing these pantomimes were.

Soon the fame of Yollande spread far and wide. She became celebrated throughout the district. Instead of asking Mother Etienne how *she* was, people asked:

"How's your hen today, Mother Etienne?"

CHAPTER IV

FATHER GUSSON'S SECRET

One day a peddler, such as often come round to villages, laden like a mule, and leading by the bridle an ass still more laden, appeared at the farm. Both looked well but tired and dusty—they seemed to have had a long journey.

Father Gusson, such was the good man's name, sold all sorts of things, from tooth-brushes to shoes,—including hardware, glassware, notions, drugs, and even patent medicines.

Mother Etienne received him kindly and after letting him show her the things in which she was interested, she offered him refreshment and suggested that he should take a little rest at the farm. This he accepted without needing any pressing.

The donkey, relieved straightway from his load, was led into the paddock, where he wallowed in the tall grass, rolling on his back, his feet in the air. He enjoyed cleaning himself up like this after his dusty journey, then, rested—he took his luncheon, choosing here and there the daintiest morsels; after which he lay down and philosophised at length.

All this time, Mother Etienne and Germaine were buying, tempted by one thing after another, silks, laces, stuffs for dresses, and a number of toilet articles, for both were, though you would not have suspected it, rather coquettish. Father Gusson—delighted with his visit to the farm and the business he had done there—was anxious to leave Mother Etienne a little remembrance.

Father Gusson the peddler comes to the farm.

"Madame," he said, holding out a small china jar carefully sealed with parchment, "assuredly you do not need this just now, but if I should never come back, and if it should happen that one day your beautiful hair should grow thin, turn grey, or fall out, you have only to rub your head with this sweet-scented ointment and at once your hair will grow again thick and of its original colour. I cannot, alas! give you the recipe, it is a secret left me by my parents."

Then Father Gusson bade farewell to the two women and went on his way with "Neddy," both much refreshed by their pleasant rest.

Mother Etienne handed Germaine the precious pot of ointment to put with their other purchases into the big cupboard, and they thought no more about it.

One day as she sat by the fire with Yollande, watching the dinner, a bright and whimsical idea occurred to the maid. "Supposing I were to try the ointment on the hen? But—it might be good for feathers too—anyhow, it could not do any harm."

Saying this she went, found the ointment, and delicately rubbed a little onto Yollande's head. Yollande did not appear to mind at all. Germaine did this three days running.

Two weeks later Mother Etienne while dressing her hen, as she did each day, found a thick reddish down sprouting round her head like a little flat wig. She showed it to Germaine, who paid no attention, having quite forgotten her childish trick.

But during the next few days the wig prospered; the hair was two finger-breadths long, very thick and curly. Mother Etienne could not understand it at all. Germaine could not, at first, make up her mind to confess to her mistress what she had done.

At last one evening, Mother Etienne being in a particularly good humour, the young girl took courage and told her all about it. Far from scolding her, her mistress was delighted, and so pleased at the news that she there and then undressed Yollande and rubbed her from head to foot with Father Gusson's marvellous ointment. She did the thing

39

thoroughly—rubbing it into every pore. Then they made a good fire so that the poor little model, thus exposed, should not take cold.

After that they watched her every instant; they were for ever undressing her to see if the cure was working—they could hardly bear to wait. Just think—if it were to succeed. It would be the end and aim of all their care. Yollande could once again take her proper place in the world.

At last what had happened to the head, happened to the body too. Before a week had gone by a thick down completely covered the big hen. The good women, much wondering, imagined that as it grew stronger the hair would change into feathers. Anxiously they awaited the change. Nothing of the sort happened. The hair remained hair—red, Titian red—fine and soft, curling round your fingers, admirable in quality and colour.

The hair on the head, older than that on the rest of the body, was much longer, which suggested to the mischievous Germaine the idea of making her an elaborate headdress.

Nothing like it had ever been seen before.

Soon Yollande was able to discard some of her clothes. Her breast and back required for a time yet a little covering, but this grew gradually less and less.

Naturally the phenomenon was much discussed in the neighbourhood, and it attracted many and delightful visitors to the farm, all of whom

Mother Etienne welcomed cordially. Yollande was less pleased with this desire to inspect her. Generally some unbeliever would tug at her hair, a painful experience for her. So, except towards her mistress and Germaine, she had become exceedingly vindictive and watchful. Every time she had the chance she pecked with her short, stout beak at the person indiscreet enough to take such liberties. One little visitor, more daring than the rest, nearly lost his finger over it.

The fame of the curly-haired hen was tremendous, it spread even beyond the limits of the district. It was really worth a journey to see her. They wrote of it in the newspapers. The "Daily Mirror," I think it was, had a fine long article about her.

But in certain quarters, the whole thing was looked upon as a "fish story."

CHAPTER V

SIR BOOUM CALLS UPON MOTHER ETIENNE

Just about this time placards were posted about the whole village, announcing the arrival of a Great American Circus, bringing in its train the most wonderful spectacles. Menageries,—curiosities of all kinds, such as had not been seen since the time of the Caesars.

Incredible things were on show. Nobody, however small their purse, could resist the pleasure of witnessing these sights. Nobody, that is, except the people in and around this village.

The menagerie prepared for its performance by splendid processions. Caparisoned in gold the elephants marched around. There were horses of all colours and of all sizes, dromedaries, rhinoceroses, black men and white monkeys, bands of musicians, fairy chariots.

The inhabitants saw the gorgeous procession pass with indifference, with a superior kind of air and without the least enthusiasm.

On the evening of the first performance, in spite of the placards, processions, bands, notices, and illuminations, nobody appeared at the ticket-office of the theatre and they played to an empty house.

"What," cried the impresario, tearing his hair. "Crowds flocked to me in London, Paris, St. Petersburg, and New York. I have been congratulated by the Shah of Persia, invited to lunch by the Grand Turk, and this little hole despises me, mocks at me, considers me a failure."

The lights out, Sir Booum spent a terrible night, wondering what evil genius could thus attack his laurels. At dawn, worn out by his sleepless night, he set out, eager to learn the cause of his failure.

All those whom he met winked knowingly, laughing in their sleeves, and courtesied to him without giving him any information. At last one, touched by his despair, answered:

"Why should we come to you? We have here in this very place, where we can see it for nothing, a marvel beside which yours are commonplace. Have you in your menagerie a curly-haired hen?"

"A curly-haired hen!" cried Sir Booum. "Gracious, goodness me! What are you talking about? Three times have I been round the world and have never heard of such a thing."

"Go to the big farm down yonder and you can see the one I am telling you about. You will be ashamed to think how uninteresting in comparison are the things you show."

A few minutes later, a magnificent equipage, driven by an elegant gentleman and drawn by two light bays, entered the courtyard of the big farm.

"Does Madame Etienne live here, please?" he asked Petit-Jacques, who was busy grooming Coco.

"Yes, sir."

"Will you kindly give her this card and ask if she will see me?"

"Certainly, sir, at once."

Petit-Jacques returned a few minutes later with Mother Etienne.

The gentleman got down from his seat, handing the reins to his groom.

"Excuse me, Madame. I am Sir Booum. It was my circus which gave its first performance here yesterday as announced on the placards posted on the walls throughout the village.

I have heard, Madame, that you have a most extraordinary hen, and I have come to beg you to show it to me. If it is really such as it was described to me, I will buy it at once."

"Sir," said Mother Etienne, "I am very pleased to meet you; I will show you Yollande as you ask, but sell her to you?—never. I love the dear thing far too well to part with her."

"But, Madame, if I give you a large sum? How much do you ask? Name your figure."

Mother Etienne, without answering a word, went off to fetch the Cochin-China hen to show to her visitor.

American as he was, he was astounded and was soon convinced that there had been no exaggeration. This was indeed the curly-haired hen.

"Well, Madame, how much is it to be?—$1,000, $2,000, $4,000? Can't you make up your mind?"

"No, sir, please don't insist. I do not want to part with dear Yollande," and Mother Etienne, distressed and trembling, covered her hen with caresses.

In vain the American urged. His eyes shone with the desire to include this marvel in his collection. He could do nothing, and was finally obliged to retreat.

"Night brings counsel, Madame. I will return tomorrow to visit you, and I hope you will then decide in my favour. Until tomorrow, then, Madame."

The gentleman bowed politely and got into his carriage. The equipage left the courtyard, turned onto the high road, and was lost in the distance in a cloud of golden dust.

CHAPTER VI

THE SEPARATION

Mother Etienne was much distressed. The unexpected appearance of this personage, the offer of this huge sum of money, were enough to excite a woman more worldly-wise than she. Germaine strove to persuade her mistress to accept the offer.

"But, my dear mistress, think of it—$4,000. It is a fortune. Don't let it escape you. It is a chance which will never come again. Think how well Yollande will be cared for. He does not mean to eat her at that price. Think of a stew costing $4,000. No indeed, the gentleman will try to keep her well as long as possible. It will be to his interest not to hurt her. Be sure of it, she will be as well cared for as she is here, if not better."

Thus they talked all evening.

Mother Etienne, feverishly affectionate, looked at the hen lying as usual asleep in the chimney corner. She could not make up her mind to sell her sweet Cinderella. Her affection for Yollande had increased with the constant care she had needed during so many long months. Besides, the silky tresses curling like corkscrews, which Germaine had kept so smooth, had been a source of amusement, not only to the farm but to the whole neighbourhood.

That night Mother Etienne was much agitated in spite of the hot drink Germaine had given her. She was haunted by a horrible nightmare. She seemed to be lying on a bed of banknotes, whilst the Cochin-China, sitting heavily on her chest, reproached her bitterly for having handed her over to a stranger in exchange for a little filthy lucre. Mother Etienne, bathed in perspiration, seemed to suffocate under her sheets.

At last dawn came, the good woman rose, her heart still terribly oppressed. Germaine calmed her as best she could with reassuring words and also with a foaming bowl of hot coffee.

All morning Mother Etienne endured torments.

It was three o'clock in the afternoon when suddenly the sound of a heavy carriage drawn by four horses was heard in the courtyard. Labric barked with all his might, Coco whinnied loudly, the three cows all mooed at the same time, and the entire poultry-yard in an uproar added its piercing and varied tones to the general tumult. The pigs especially made a great noise.

It was the American's four-in-hand.

He was driving himself, and on his left sat a young and pretty woman, exquisitely dressed in white.

The newcomers were at once shown into the huge kitchen, which served also as a reception room. On the hearth burned a small bundle of scented herbs which filled the whole room with fragrance. Yollande was sitting in her usual place.

"Well, Madame, have you at last decided to let me have the curly-haired hen?"

Mother Etienne neither moved nor answered.

"See here, Madame, I offer you $4,000, $6,000, $8,000," and so saying he took from a red morocco pocketbook in banknotes the sums he mentioned, and spread them out on the table before the astonished eyes of Mother Etienne and Germaine.

Mother Etienne still shook her head in refusal.

Germaine, driven wild by this sight, began to exclaim: "Yes, sir,—yes, Madame. Yes, sir,—yes, Madame," and threw herself into the arms first of the American, and then of Mother Etienne, who still remained obdurate.

Miss Booum, taking Mother Etienne's hand, said coaxingly: "You can safely trust her to me. I will take care of her myself, Madame. With us she will become famous throughout the world. All the newspapers will speak of her. From your poultry-yard she will come into contact with the greatest courts of the world. She will be petted by Grand Duchesses, and receive hands. Besides all this she will be in good company and will have plenty to amuse her."

This pleading succeeded in dragging from Mother Etienne the longed-for "Yes," which, though stifled by emotion, was seized upon by the American.

The good woman had said "Yes," she had conquered the selfishness of a mother for two reasons. She did not want to prevent Yollande from getting on in the world, and also she wished to let Germaine share this fortune, for it was owing to her that the hen had become so valuable, and she did not think it right to deprive her of the benefit.

Miss Booum brings Mother Etienne to the circus tent.

"That's all settled, then. Here's the contract," said the American, "you have only to sign it." And a receipt duly prepared was handed to Mother Etienne, who in a trembling hand appended her signature and a flourish. I don't know that she did not even embellish it with a huge blot of ink.

Then Miss Booum stooped and gently took under her arm Yollande, who oddly enough made no resistance.

"Oh please, please let me kiss her again," and, tears in her eyes, Mother Etienne tenderly embraced the Cochin-China.

"You will take great care of Yollande, won't you? You will send me news of her? Where is she to sleep tonight?"

"Oh, as to that, Madame, would you like to see the place prepared for her? Come with us. There is room in the carriage and I promise to have you brought back again at once. The camp is not far from here, the road is good, the horses fast, and in half an hour at most you will be perfectly reassured and can return with your mind at rest."

Mother Etienne, without further thought, still guided by her tender maternal heart, needed no urging, but followed by the two Americans, walked with a brisk, firm step towards the carriage. Suddenly changing her mind, she said:

"Will you just let me change my dress? I can't very well go out like this."

She went to her room, an idea having entered her head, and soon returned very neatly dressed with a little basket in her hand.

The steps were adjusted and the three people took their places on top, whilst Yollande, wrapped in soft woollen covers, was carefully placed inside, in a basket provided for that very purpose.

When Germaine saw her mistress start off she would have liked to go with her, but the farm needed her attention. Besides, Miss Booum's promise of seats for the next performance quite consoled her.

The carriage made a curve in the yard, went through the gate, and soon disappeared, bearing the two new travellers. As Miss Booum had said, it did not take more than half an hour to reach the camp, the cobs went so quickly.

On the way Mother Etienne met many acquaintances to whom she waved a simple but cordial greeting. In most cases the carriage was already out of sight before they recovered sufficiently from their astonishment to wave back.

It was a nine days' wonder.

CHAPTER VII

SIR BOOUM'S CIRCUS

Our travellers came in sight of the circus. Imagine, children, a huge encampment like a small town,—with sections, and streets, houses of green canvas on stout poles, tall caravans on wheels enclosing everything as though with impassable walls, and in the centre all sorts of people, in all sorts of costumes, walking up and down.

There were brown men, yellow men, red men, black men, big men, little men, thin men, fat men, lame men, deformed men, men with goitres, men covered with feathers, men covered with fur,—in fact, men of every possible kind, size, and land,—men to suit every possible taste.

All the most curious specimens were represented. Besides these there was a colossal menagerie. In it there were more than twenty elephants, giraffes, hippopotami, rhinoceroses, zebras, dromedaries, camels, and the rarest kinds of antelopes. Then came the reptiles,—from the boa constrictor, who was ten yards long, to the smallest blind-worm, amongst them some of the most dangerous kinds. Crocodiles twenty feet long, monstrous toads, tortoises as big as donkeys. Then there were the wild beasts too. Lions from Abyssinia, from Atlas, tigers from Bengal, from Persia, jaguars, panthers, leopards, all the big cat family, lynx, onca, tiger cat. Bears of all kinds, grizzly, grey, black, and white. Then came wolves, foxes, coyotes, in fact the whole series of the dog tribe with every possible domestic variety.

In little barred cages was a collection of smaller carnivorous animals and rodents. In a huge room all the monkeys from the big gorilla to the minute ouistiti or witsit, were installed; they squabbled, pulled one another's tails, bit one another, uttered piercing cries. There were constant battles going on in that corner.

Then in an immense aviary were all the birds of creation, divided into classes, from the humming-bird, the size of a hornet, to the ostrich. This was, to tell the truth, the part that interested Mother Etienne most of all. She was more used to creatures of this kind, they reminded her of her beloved poultry-yard. In spite of the signs put up everywhere, "Do not feed the animals," the good woman who had purposely filled her basket with cakes threw them in indiscriminately. There were enough for all the animals she passed. First she threw some to the lions. The lions took no notice, at which she was most surprised. Her idea in offering the cakes was to see if the animals were hungry and to find out that way how they were treated.

Miss Booum, who was acting as her guide, was much amused at her astonishment and could not resist saying:

"Madame, to offer a cream bun to a tiger is like offering a beef-steak to an elephant. Just keep your cakes for the ostriches, they are so greedy that they will eat stones. If they were to keep a hardware store they would be certain to eat up their stock."

Pleased at this permission, when she came to the ostriches, Mother Etienne offered them a cake, but they looked down at it very haughtily and suspiciously. From this she concluded that even those birds were so well-fed that they were not hungry and felt quite satisfied about Yollande.

After half an hour's walk through the circus, having visited every corner of it, they went towards the manager's house. There five o'clock tea was served. Mother Etienne, quite at ease, did honour to the lunch so graciously provided, and after thanking Miss Booum gratefully, she kissed Yollande very tenderly and prepared to return to the farm.

At a sign from the young American girl, a stout piebald pony, harnessed to a trap, was led forward by a groom.

"That is my own carriage and my horse Charlie, which you can drive yourself, Madame, if you like. He is quick and safe, you may be sure of that. You will be at home again in less time than it took to come here with four horses. Farewell, dear Madame, a pleasant drive. Remember that we expect you tomorrow for the afternoon performance, and that nice little maid of yours too. Your seats will be reserved."

The two women shook hands cordially, Mother Etienne got into the carriage, and took the reins. The pony feeling a hand used to driving, set off at a quick trot, then warming to his work flew over the ground. He had the paces of a big horse and had to be kept well in hand.

Mother Etienne soon reached home delighted with her adventure. She was assailed by questions from Germaine and Petit-Jacques. They sat there drinking in her words. Mother Etienne told them as best she could all that had happened and all that she had seen in the most secret wings of the gigantic circus. Germaine in her excitement was forgetful enough to let the soup boil over and the roast burn, but all the same they dined gaily. There were still plenty of questions to be asked. Mother Etienne had to go over every detail and even to tell some stories over again. They went on talking far into the night—so charmed were the listeners at the recital.

Nobody thought of going to bed. Germaine was longing for the morrow, she was so anxious to see for herself this fairyland.

At last, midnight striking, reminded Mother Etienne that it was time for sleep. Then they all went to bed, each head full of the wonders of tomorrow's performance.

CHAPTER VIII

MOTHER ETIENNE'S DREAM

Mother Etienne was very restless again that night, haunted, not by a dreadful nightmare as before, but by a troublesome dream. Everything she had just seen at Sir Booum's appeared before her, the tiniest incidents, the least important details.

All the explanations, concerning the creatures in the menagerie given her by the trainer, came back to her, like an object lesson in a curious dream.

The principal person in it was Yollande. Yollande as Barnum, Yollande as trainer, Yollande holding in one hairy wing a stout whip, in the other the pitchfork as a protection against claws and teeth.

"You see here," said Yollande in a loud voice, "you see here the wild ox from Madagascar, which takes the place of the horse. In that country he is harnessed to small, light vehicles which he draws along rapidly. This other is a buffalo from Caffraria. He is a Jack-of-all-trades, sometimes ridden, sometimes driven, sometimes laden, sometimes yoked to the plough. Those big striped animals you see yonder are giraffes. Their long necks permit them, without having recourse to a ladder, to eat the young shoots of the mimosa, of which they are very fond, as well as the fresh dates which usually grow at the tops of the palm-trees."

In this kind of dream a strange idea was at work in the brain of the sleeper. With these object lessons were mingled strange, quaint asides.

"If children had long necks like that, one couldn't keep the jam-pots out of their way by putting them on the top shelves of the cupboard."

"There," went on Yollande, "are the elephants. They are used for all sorts of tasks. Their trunks, a continuation of their nostrils, serve both for breathing and holding. It is, as it were, an extremely sensitive and powerful hand."

"Great goodness me," cried Mother Etienne; "imagine having a hand at the end of your nose! Would it have a glove on it and rings on its fingers?"

All sorts of ridiculous ideas like that came into her head. The little beaver, who builds his houses all along the Canadian streams, appeared trowel in hand, mortar-board on his head, and Mother Etienne felt most anxious to have his valuable assistance in repairing her barns and mills. Dear little marabout, how useful you would be in the village, sweeping the streets, cleaning up the refuse, advance-guard of the street-cleaner with his, "Now then, everything into the gutter."

"The antelopes are very silly, coquettish creatures to wear such long boas round their necks in this warm country. But, after all, perhaps they are wise enough, for they have chosen a kind which, unlike our make of furs, is cold to the touch."

Yollande, in her rôle of trainer, went on and on like a brook.

"Here, now, is a dromedary. He has a hump on his back, a fatty exerescence which enables him to bear much fatigue, without eating or drinking for several days. It is owing to this fat, rather like a box of provisions on his back, that he can traverse hot and sandy deserts where it would be difficult to find a single blade of grass to eat."

Then through the farm bedroom passed long caravans of camels, led by carnival Arabs, their humps changed into gigantic larders in which rattled all sorts of canned things. Canned salmon, Russian caviare, dried biscuits, smoked meats, tongues, sardines, canned peas, foies-gras, lobsters, and fruits, in fact all those things which Mother Etienne had seen piled up in many-coloured pyramids at the best grocery stores. Really it was too ridiculous.—Miss Booum must have been making fun of her visitor.—That couldn't really be the best food for camels.

It was still worse when it came to the turn of the hippopotami. A thousand ill-digested memories from the illustrated papers were in her mind, all mixed up. Where did the Nile and the Zanzibar flow? Which was it that separated Egypt from Senegal? And the gigantic hippopotamus, looking perfectly huge and out-of-place in a gondola fit for a sultana, appeared to her, floating down the calm stream, a red fez with a golden star on his head, puffing away at a peculiar double-bowled pipe, the pride of the collection of a retired police-officer in the village, who had it from the real cousin of a sea-captain from Marseilles.

"Do you see those little lumps there enclosed between four boards? It is a nest of land-tortoises. The largest, called the Giant tortoise, easily supports on its back a weight of two hundred pounds. This shell which weighs so heavily is its house. At the least alarm, it retreats into its house and stays there, till all danger is past." This plan of walking about with your house on your back seemed rather a good one to Mother Etienne. You could go out on rainy days without getting wet, and on cold days it would keep your back nice and warm.

"Near at hand is a collection of mammals, the kangaroo family. The kangaroo is the largest mammal of Australia. It is generally a peace-loving animal, but bites, scratches, and claws if it is teased. Its best defence however is flight." All these technical details left the good woman cold. What she remembered best were the practical qualities of the creatures. The kangaroo has one very great peculiarity, the female has a pouch, a sort of bag, in which she hides her young if danger appears, just as the soldier has his knapsack.

For the first time in her life Mother Etienne was much struck By certain resemblances between animals and human beings, finding in them actions, looks, and habits which reminded her irresistibly of many of her acquaintances. It was amongst the monkeys that it was the most marked. Two chimpanzees, with pensive faces garbed in black, seemed to be mourning some beloved relative. It was as though their sad but shining eyes, gazing at the straw which half-covered them, were seeking something hidden, intangible.

A family of big African monkeys, by their challenging, crafty air, reminded her unpleasantly of a band of good-for-nothings who for months had spread terror and desolation throughout the country. The chief—or the one who appeared to be the chief—the biggest and strongest, hurled himself at the bars and shook them in his clenched hands. He would certainly have enjoyed strangling Mother Etienne, had he been able to do so. Since he was not able to, he displayed in a huge yawn, a terrifying set of teeth, worthy of a wild beast. They were horrid animals, I assure you, not the kind you would like to meet loose on a lonely road.

Fortunately some pretty little witsits, with black faces, no bigger than your fist, and white and grey ruffles, whistling like blackbirds, by their pretty tricks did away with the bad impression made by these sinister neighbours.

Cake Walk; Mother Etienne's dream.

This one was a regular little mother, that one had just been sweeping out the yard, another was the living image of the Count's servant when he followed his master on his walks, carrying under his arm a shawl or a sunshade. An orang-outang, an elderly peasant, whose four big hands were clasped, suggested to her how useful it would be to have a helper like that to milk the cows. It would go twice as fast with four hands. What a lot of precious time it would save.

And many other queer things came into her head. That yowling dog, that sharp-faced rabbit, are the type who come on fair-days to cry their papers, sell their toys, etc.—a noisy, rough crew. Goodness gracious! Where was Mother Etienne's absurd dream leading her? She, whose life was always so calm, and who, to tell the truth, with Germaine, were rather like the two little monkeys at the corner of the fire-place, hands clasped under their aprons, feet on foot-warmers, and little pointed handkerchiefs on their heads.

At this personal picture everything turned as though by enchantment into one huge, vast medley, which ended in a general cake-walk of the whole menagerie, passing before the tired eyes of Mother Etienne, roaring, bellowing, mewing, whistling, howling, whinnying, and braying. Poor Mother Etienne was thoroughly exhausted.

CHAPTER IX

MOTHER ETIENNE'S FORTUNE

When she woke up the good woman thought of her small fortune. She gave it for safe keeping into the hands of her lawyer, M. La Plume, while she was making up her mind how she should dispose of it. She wanted plenty of time to think it over. She had already decided to give Germaine a dowry, for the whole thing was largely owing to her. She knew that she and Petit-Jacques were in love.

"They will make a fine couple," she thought, "and later on how pleased I shall be to have a nice family around me—with dear children who will love and care for me."

Then she thought of Père Gusson—the good old man could have no idea of all that had happened at the farm. He was going his rounds, selling his wares as best he could. It was three months since he had appeared, he would be back again before long—he had already been away longer than usual.

And, sure enough, two days later Neddy announced his entrance into the courtyard with a loud bray. If his master was glad to see Mother Etienne who always received him so cordially, and who bought so much from him, the donkey fully appreciated the hours of rest and the good food he found in the paddock with the cows.

Mother Etienne went forward to meet the old man and gaily told him the whole story.

He, utterly astounded, could not at first believe it. He made her repeat the wonder over and over again. It certainly was a very curious thing. He had always known his ointment was effective, but—as to making hair grow on a hen—that was quite another thing. He was just petrified by it.

Mother Etienne told Germaine to serve some good cider, and all three drank to one another's healths.

"That is not all," said Mother Etienne, "I want you to have a share in my good fortune. That's only fair. You have worked all your life, you must think of taking a rest. You have certainly earned it. Here is a check for $2,000 which my lawyer, M. La Plume, will cash for you. This sum, together with what you have saved, will be enough to buy a little house and garden and to keep you from want. If one is wise and knows how to manage, one can live here for very little."

Father Gusson, quite upset and touched, could not find words to thank dear, kind Mother Etienne. It was as though he had unexpectedly won the big prize in the lottery. He could hardly believe his eyes and ears.

Soon he pulled himself together and began to calculate.

"I have a few savings, it is true, but I think it would be wise to take advantage of the fame of the ointment and double my small fortune.

I hope that, thanks to the already widespread fame of Yollande, if (with your kind permission) I were to call my ointment, 'Ointment of the Curly-Haired Hen' I should have considerable success."

"Not only am I quite willing, but I thoroughly approve of your idea and strongly advise you to carry it out," replied Mother Etienne warmly.

No sooner said than done.

Father Gusson withdrew from the notary the sum, so fairly But generously given him, and spent his time henceforth in manufacturing (according to the recipe of his ancestors) the wonderful ointment. He filled a great quantity of jars of all sizes, and like the good business man he was, having adorned them with magnificent labels he doubled the price of the ointment and put on a trade mark so as to prohibit imitations. Then he bought a cart like Mother Etienne's and harnessed Neddy to it. On the hood of the cart was a huge picture of a Curly-Haired Hen, and under it was the inscription, "Ointment of the Curly-Haired Hen." Now the peddler could go his rounds, selling only this specialty, without need of further advertisement. The effect was magic. Doors, hitherto too often closed against him, opened wide at his coming and there was not a soul who did not buy quite a lot of it.

In a month and without effort, Father Gusson took in ten times more money than he had earned in all his long and hardworking life before.

CHAPTER X

TRIUMPH OF THE OINTMENT

The craze of the public for this new preparation was extraordinary. A china factory, about to close its doors, made a fortune out of manufacturing jars for it. Of course all the bald people bought it. Everyone expected it to work miracles. The women with tow-coloured rat-tails expected to grow luxuriant black tresses and others with coarse scrubby black hair dreamed of having fine soft golden braids.

A very rich land-owner, who did not care how much he spent, rubbed with it the back of his mangy dog, and his horse's tail, which was growing somewhat thin.

The mayor even, they tell me, put a thick layer of it onto his wig, which was beginning to wear out. The district was steeped in it, the air seemed to smell of musk.

Alas! everything has its bad side. The good side of this was for the merchant alone, who, though he guaranteed his wares for human beings, refused any further responsibility. The bad side was for the hens and ducks. (I believe even the geese suffered occasionally.) I can't tell you how many people, knowing all about the effect it had had on Yollande and the resultant fortune, tried to duplicate the famous Curly-Haired Hen, bought by Sir Booum.

In the poultry-yards around, the hens for several months had a pretty bad time. They were nearly all plucked and rubbed with the ointment. It was a craze, a rage with the farmers, and those hens who could retain a vestige of their plumage esteemed themselves fortunate.

It was a sad sight to see all the feathered creatures fly at the sight of a human being. They knew by bitter experience what to expect. Alas! with all these attempts with roosters, chickens, ducks, and turkeys, none had the desired effect. They long remained scented and devoid of plumage, that was all. We must take it that no subject as good as Yollande presented itself. Nature makes these queer incomprehensible distinctions, you know, which we just can't understand. There was *one* Curly-Haired Hen, there was to be no other! For, since her metamorphosis, for a reason unknown to this day, the Curly-Haired Hen absolutely refused to lay eggs. This was, I must confess, a great disappointment to Sir Booum. Like the good American he was, he would have liked to continue the race.

He had perforce to content himself with portraits of her from the pen of M. Vimar. One of these was sent, affectionately dedicated by Yollande, to her good Mother Etienne, who regards it as her greatest treasure, and keeps it, elegantly framed, above the mantelpiece in her bedroom. Never a day passes but the good woman looks at it with tender, motherly affection.

Father Gusson is now the owner of a pretty little house and cultivates his own garden, in which is a corner reserved for Neddy, for he too has earned his rest.

Germaine, to whom her mistress and adopted mother gave a good dowry, has just married Petit-Jacques, quartermaster, lately returned from his military service.

It is hard to tell which is the happiest. The wedding was performed with much ceremony. The whole village was present, and amongst the various healths drunk they did not omit that of the "Curly-Haired Hen."

Love animals, my children, be kind to them, care for them, you will certainly have your reward.

FINIS

Lightning Source UK Ltd.
Milton Keynes UK
UKHW021419121120
373269UK00004B/174